For...
Jorgenson & Foster,...
Have a wonderful Christmas!
2012

The Fish Tank

Other Schiffer Books By The Author:

Sam: The Tale of a Chesapeake Bay Rockfish, 978-0-87033-499-3, $10.95

ISBN: 978-0-7643-3706-2
Printed in China

Schiffer Books are available at special discounts for bulk purchases for sales promotions or premiums. Special editions, including personalized covers, corporate imprints, and excerpts can be created in large quantities for special needs. For more information contact the publisher:

Published by Schiffer Publishing Ltd.
4880 Lower Valley Road
Atglen, PA 19310
Phone: (610) 593-1777; Fax: (610) 593-2002
E-mail: Info@schifferbooks.com

For the largest selection of fine reference books on this and related subjects,

please visit our web site at **www.schifferbooks.com**
We are always looking for people to write books on new and related subjects. If you have an idea for a book please contact us at the above address.

This book may be purchased from the publisher.
Include $5.00 for shipping.
Please try your bookstore first.

You may write for a free catalog.

In Europe, Schiffer books are distributed by
Bushwood Books
6 Marksbury Ave.
Kew Gardens
Surrey TW9 4JF England
Phone: 44 (0) 20 8392 8585; Fax: 44 (0) 20 8392 9876
E-mail: info@bushwoodbooks.co.uk
Website: www.bushwoodbooks.co.uk

The Fish Tank

Kristina Henry

Illustrated by Laura Ambler and Amanda Brown

Schiffer Publishing Ltd

4880 Lower Valley Road Atglen, Pennsylvania 19310

Printed in China

For Allegra, Konradt, and Saskia with love from Aunt Tina

Big Orange Goldfish
Has a fantail with a hole.
He swims back and forth.

Tetra is so small.
She hides in a pink castle.
Often she's afraid.

Tiger Barbs swim fast!
Biting, chasing other fish.
Mainly Big Goldfish.

Angelfish stays veiled.
Safe behind filter bubbles.
Not so nice, this tank.

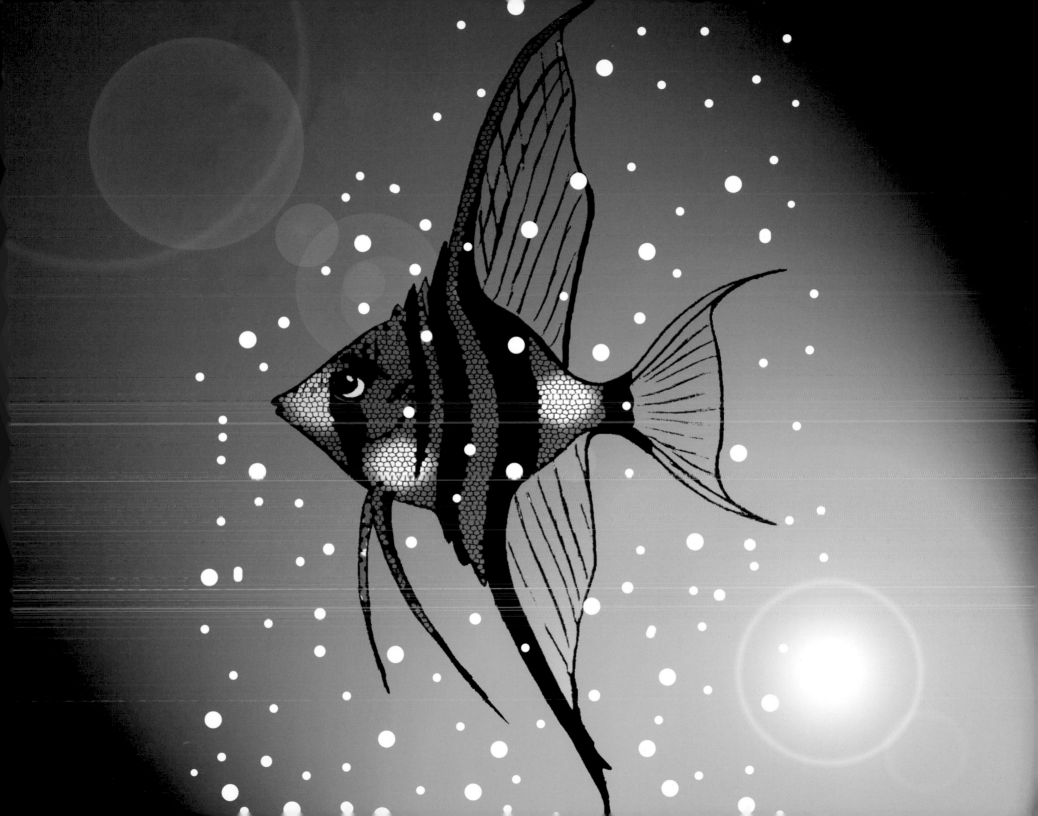

The tank *is* roomy.
There's a castle and tall plants.
Lots of space to swim.

But water's murky.
Fish can't see. They guard their turf.
Friend? Foe? Who knows which?

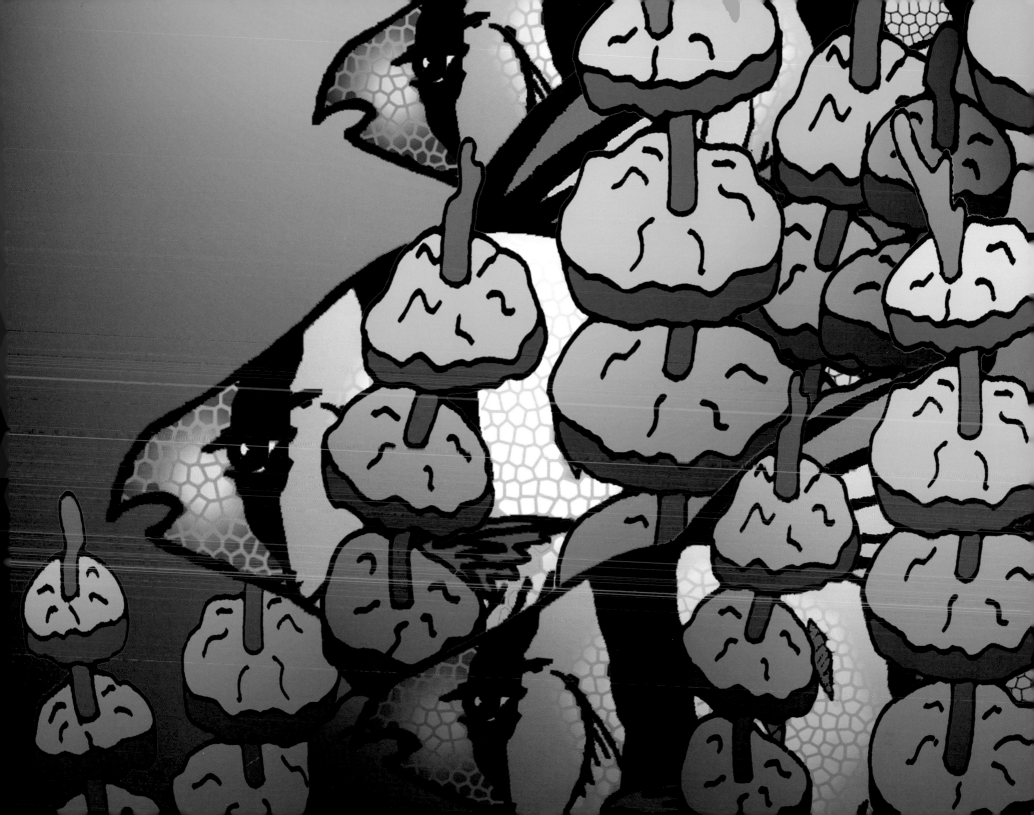

So many colors
Hidden by cloudy water.
Pretty fish look plain.

All can share this world.
Don't start off on the wrong fin.
Fish will strike, get hurt.

Hiding's easier.
Fighting all the time is tough.
Scales drop off. Tails droop.

What is that up top?
A newcomer, quiet, brown,
Sliding down real slow.

Makes a shiny streak.
Wow! The tank has one clean stripe.
Fish stop and watch. Cool.

Tiger Barbs don't see.
They still chase and bite. It's war!
Other fish leave quick!

Goldfish bumps tetra.
Tetra's instincts say, "Go now!"
Tiger Barbs divide.

Goldfish hides in plants.
Tetra rushes for castle.
Angelfish swims off.

Nighttime comes. Fish wait.
It's dark. Scary. All is still.
Filter hums softly.

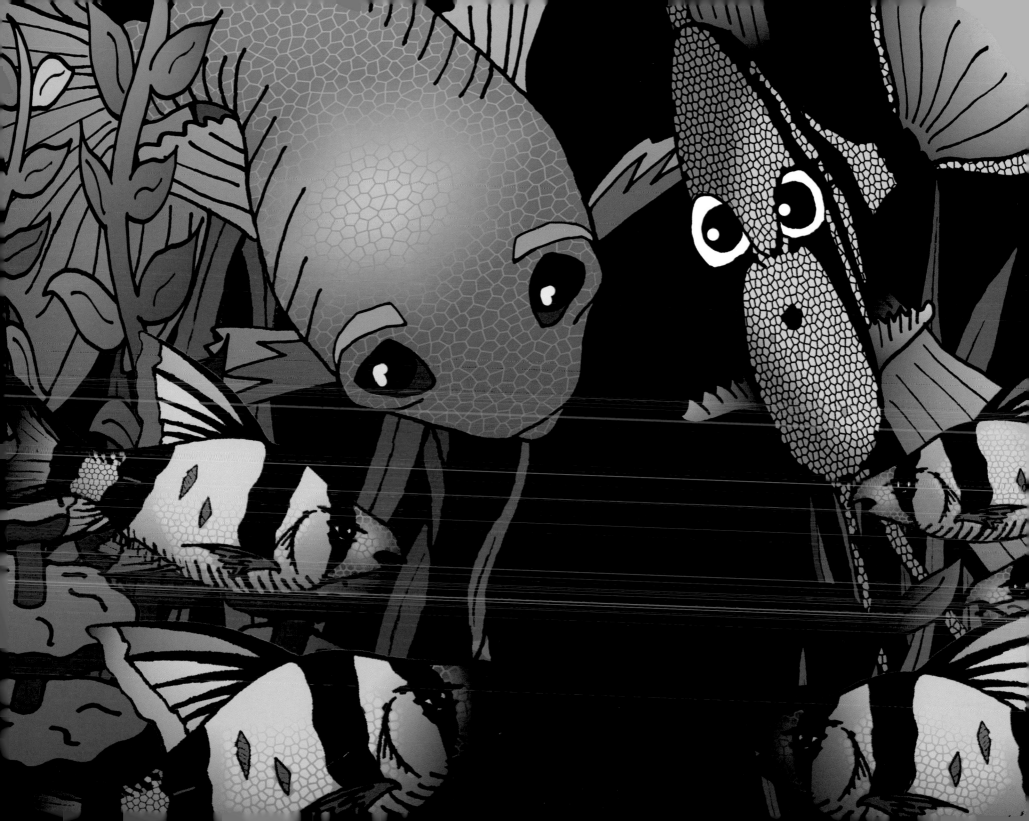

Fish stay alert. Watch.
Tank life is much too stressful.
All are so tired.

Morning's here. It's bright.
Fish marvel at their new home.
Snail's cleanup complete.

Tank sparkles. Fish shine.
Even Tiger Barbs don't chase.
All is beautiful.

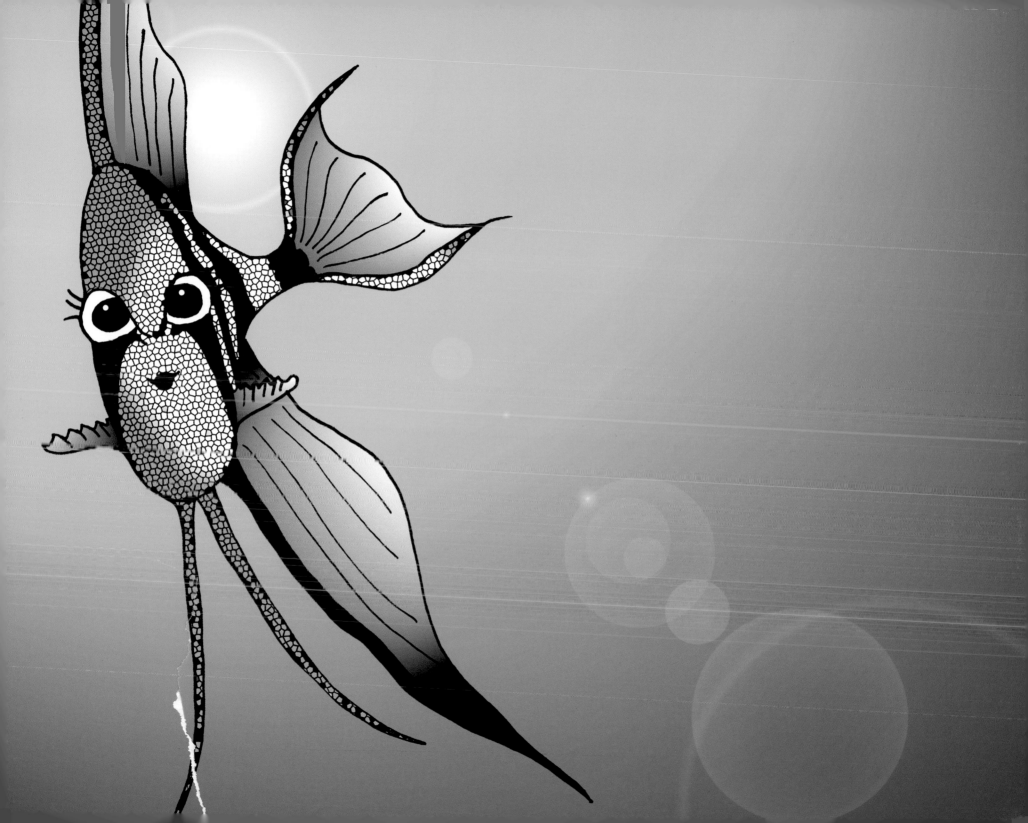

Now snail keeps things clean.
Fish swim above and below.
No need to fight, hide.

A happy clean home.
Lots of light and room to move.
At last life is good.

About the Author

Kristina Henry's writing has appeared in *The Washington Post* and *The Washingtonian* magazine. She is also the author of *Sam: The Tale of a Chesapeake Bay Rockfish*. She lives with her husband, Mike, in Easton, Maryland.

About the Illustrators

Laura Ambler is proof that you don't need to leave home to reinvent yourself. The former Telly Award winning advertising executive was bored in her industry and looking for something new to stir her creative juices. In 1998 she enrolled in a screenwriting class offered at Johns Hopkins University and a year later had launched a career in Hollywood—without ever leaving her hometown of Easton, Maryland.

Ambler is a member of the Writer's Guild of America East and has written approximately twenty screenplays, including *The White Pony,* produced by legendary producer and director, Roger Corman. She also wrote and produced the children's videos *Horses A to Z, Airplanes A to Z,* and *I Love Horses.*

Amanda Brown was born and raised on the Eastern Shore of Maryland. Her illustrations have appeared in *The Fish Tank*, *The Turtle Tank*, and the *Rat Tank*. She currently lives with two crazy kittens, Zero and Yukki, in Easton, Maryland, where she attends a local college. In her spare time, Amanda enjoys cooking, sewing, and drawing comics about her friends.